Get that Broom!
and
Fizz! Wizz!

Maverick
Early Readers

'Get that Broom!' and 'Fizz! Wizz!'
An original concept by Katie Dale
© Katie Dale

Illustrated by Lindsay Dale-Scott

Published by MAVERICK ARTS PUBLISHING LTD
Studio 11, City Business Centre, 6 Brighton Road,
Horsham, West Sussex, RH13 5BB
© Maverick Arts Publishing Limited November 2019
+44 (0)1403 256941

A CIP catalogue record for this book is available at the British Library.

ISBN 978-1-84886-627-0

www.maverickbooks.co.uk

This book is rated as: Red Band (Guided Reading)
This story is decodable at Letters and Sounds Phase 2.

Get that Broom!
and
Fizz! Wizz!

By **Katie Dale**

Illustrated by
Lindsay Dale-Scott

The Letter B

Trace the lower and upper case letter with a finger. Sound out the letter.

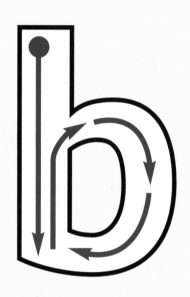

Down,
up,
around

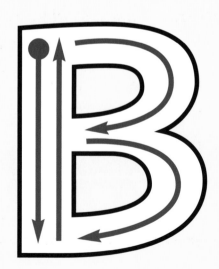

Down,
up,
around,
around

Some words to familiarise:

Otter Chimp Panda

High-frequency words:

to   the   on   you

Tips for Reading 'Get that Broom!'

- Practise the words listed above before reading the story.

- If the reader struggles with any of the other words, ask them to look for sounds they know in the word. Encourage them to sound out the words and help them read the words if necessary.

- After reading the story, ask the reader how Elephant was able to stop the broom.

Fun Activity

Discuss what other animals could stop the broom.

Get that Broom!

Nell zooms to the zoo.

Cat gets on the broom.

Zoom, zoom, zoom!

7

Otter gets the broom.
Zoom, zoom, zoom!

Chimp gets the broom.
Zoom, zoom, zoom!

Panda gets the broom.
Zoom, zoom, zoom!

Elephant gets the broom.
The broom cannot zoom!

Nell gets on the broom.
Zoom, zoom, zoom!

The Letter F

Trace the lower and upper case letter with a finger. Sound out the letter.

*Around,
down,
lift,
cross*

*Down,
lift,
cross,
lift,
cross*

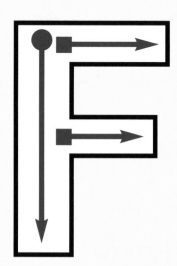

Some words to familiarise:

bun   plum   fish

High-frequency words:

I   a   said   was   you

Tips for Reading 'Fizz! Wizz!'

- Practise the words listed above before reading the story.

- If the reader struggles with any of the other words, ask them to look for sounds they know in the word. Encourage them to sound out the words and help them read the words if necessary.

- After reading the story, ask the reader why Frog got ill.

Fun Activity

What snack would you wish for?

Fizz! Wizz!

"I wish I had a snack," said Nell.

Fizz! Wizz!

"I wish I had a bun," said Rat.

Fizz! Wizz!

"I wish I had a plum," said Bat.

Fizz! Wizz!

"I wish I had a fish," said Cat.

"I wish I had a bug," said Frog.

Fizz! Wizz!

Ribbit!

"I wish Frog was well," said Nell.

Fizz! Wizz!

Book Bands for Guided Reading

The Institute of Education book banding system is a scale of colours that reflects the various levels of reading difficulty. The bands are assigned by taking into account the content, the language style, the layout and phonics. Word, phrase and sentence level work is also taken into consideration.

Maverick Early Readers are a bright, attractive range of books covering the pink to white bands. All of these books have been book banded for guided reading to the industry standard and edited by a leading educational consultant.

Pink
Red
Yellow
Blue
Green
Orange
Turquoise
Purple
Gold
White

To view the whole Maverick Readers scheme, visit our website at
www.maverickearlyreaders.com

Or scan the QR code above to view our scheme instantly!